BAXTER BARRET BROWN'S COWBOY BAND

BY TIM A. MCKENZIE ♫ ILLUSTRATIONS by F

This is BAXTER BARRET BROWN and his BASS FIDDLE

Baxter loved to play his big bass fiddle with the cowboys on TV.

One day, he decided that it would be fun to play music with real cowboys at a real ranch. So...

he pulled on his boots,
strapped on his spurs,
saddled his horse,
tied on his
bass fiddle...

and off to the ranch he rode.

At the ranch, when Baxter asked
if he could play some cowboy songs
with some real cowboys,
the foreman said,
"We'd love to,
but we can't
right now.
We have
to find a
way to
brand the cattle. The cowboys left
the branding irons in the fire too long,
and they all melted.

He took off one of his **big bass fiddle strings** and formed it into a brand. He heated it in the fire, and he and the cowboys went to work.

When the branding was all done, Baxter asked the ranch foreman again if they could play some cowboy songs.

The foreman said, "We'd love to, but we can't right now. Our chuckwagon is broken down, and we can't carry our dinner to the north pasture.

We're behind schedule, and we won't have any use for a **big bass fiddle** on a wild west cattle drive."

Baxter ran to get his **bass fiddle branding iron.**

He mounted the chuckwagon wheels on the bottom of his **bass fiddle**, put a canvas cover on top, hitched up a team of horses, **and off he went...**

thinking about
how much fun
they would have
playing cowboy songs
when the trail drive
was over.

When they arrived
at the north pasture,
Baxter was ready to play
some cowboy songs with some
real cowboys. But the foreman
said, "We can't do that now because
we have to find a way to water the
cattle. The windmill has blown down,
and the water tank is dry.
I don't think we have any use for a
big bass fiddle up in the north pasture when
there's no water for the cattle."

Baxter

an to get his bass fiddle chuckwagon.

BAXTER took the neck off his **bass fiddle** and used it to repair the windmill. He took off the front and started the windmill turning and pumping until it filled up his bass with enough water to give all the cattle plenty to drink.

There was even enough water for the cowboys to take a bath.

That evening, Baxter wanted to play cowboy songs around the campfire, but everyone was too tired. The foreman said, "We don't have any use for a **big bass fiddle** in the north pasture at bedtime."

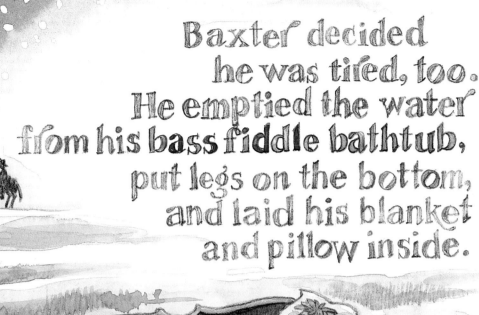

Baxter decided
he was tired, too.
He emptied the water
from his **bass fiddle bathtub**,
put legs on the bottom,
and laid his blanket
and pillow inside.

Then he settled down by the fire, listening to the sounds of the prairie animals and a yodeling cowboy singing to the herd.

The next morning, Baxter woke up to the **rumble of thunder**. The foreman said, "A storm washed out the bridge, and there's no way to get across the creek."

Baxter ran to get his **bass fiddle bed**.

He laid it down where the bridge used to be.

One by one, all the cows and cowboys crossed over the creek safely.

When they all arrived back at the bunkhouse, they saw a great big cattle truck driving through the front gate.

The cowboys said, "Oh, NO! More cows!"

The foreman said, "There were so many uses for a **big bass fiddle** on a wild west trail drive, that I got one for everybody at the ranch."

BIG BASS FIDDLE RANCH

Now all of the cowboys use big bass fiddles everywhere they go. They even changed the name of the ranch to **BIG BASS FIDDLE RANCH.**

The foreman said, "It's time for **Baxter** to play
All the cowboys gathered 'round on the
Finally, **Baxter** was able to play cowboy
songs with some real cowboys.

He decided

ome music on his **big bass fiddle**."
unkhouse porch.

le loved the sounds all the other instruments made.

hat he wanted to play them, but he couldn't decide which one. So...

The End

BRIGHT SKY PRESS

Box 416
Albany, Texas 76430

10 9 8 7 6 5 4 3 2 1

Library of Congress Cataloging-in-Publication Data

McKenzie, Tim A., 1956–
    Baxter Barret Brown's cowboy band / by Tim A. McKenzie ; illustrations by Elaine Atkinson.
        p. cm.
    Summary: Baxter Barret Brown hopes to play his bass fiddle with a real cowboy band on a ranch but when branding irons melt and the chuckwagon breaks down, Baxter discovers never-before-imagined uses for his instrument.
    ISBN-13: 978-1-931721-77-6 (hardcover : alk. paper) [1. Cowboys—Fiction. 2. Double bass—Fiction. 3. Ranch life—Fiction.] I. Atkinson, Elaine, ill. II. Title.

PZ7.M4786762Bbc 2006
[E]—dc22

                                          2006045498

Cover design by Isabel Lasater Hernandez

Printed in China through Asia Pacific Offset